The Little Book of
POT

The Little Book of

POT

DR V.S. GANJABHANG

BⒷXTREE

First published 2001 by Boxtree
an imprint of Pan Macmillan Ltd
Pan Macmillan, 20 New Wharf Road, London N1 9RR
Basingstoke and Oxford
Associated companies throughout the world
www.panmacmillan.com

ISBN-13: 978-0-7522-6174-4
ISBN-10: 0-7522-6174-6

10

A CIP catalogue record for this book is available from
the British Library.

Typeset by Dan Newman/Perfect Bound Ltd
Printed by The Bath Press, Bath

Ganja, Marijuana – call it what you will, it's illegal and you shouldn't be doing it. However, millions of people do and they remain some of the most creative, incisive, sleepy and chronically hungry members of society. What other drug could have influenced both Bob Marley and Dylan from the Magic Roundabout, or inspired such crucial advances as the Wagon Wheel or the Metallica T-Shirt?

Pot has no adverse side effects (apart from the medical ones, obviously) and has been scientifically proven to improve your sex appeal (albeit only to other junkies.) It is a 10,000 year old industry as fascinating as the people who use it and significantly more productive.

In short, this book is all about Pot.

Contents

Ganja Glossary

Pot/Dope/Shit/Hash/Cake

Generic slang for dried cannabis resin.

Grass/Ganja/Weed/Tweed

Generic slang for dried cannabis leaves, flowers or buds.

Sensimilia/Skunk/Chronic
Common types of grass.

Hemp
The root, stalk and stems of the cannabis plant, widely used for making rope, fabric (the word 'canvas' is derived from cannabis), oil and, of course, Green Rizlas.

Spliff/Blunt/Joint/Rollie
Cannabis cigarette.

Dealer

1. A trader in narcotics, traditionally distinguished by his jolly cry of 'Who will buy this wonderful shit? One shilling a bag!'

2. An untrustworthy little bastard who would sell his own mother if she could be divided into 1oz quantities.

Roach

A handmade filter inserted into one end of a joint.

Pothead/dopehead

An aspiring junkie. Sober enough to know he has a problem, too stoned to do anything about it.

Marijuana

1930s Mexican slang for cannabis. The original lyrics of 'La Cucaracha' tell of a Mexican soldier who refuses to fight until he is given more marijuana.

Rastafarian/Rasta

1. Religious follower of Haile Selassie, former Emperor of Ethiopia.

2. Permanently stoned Jamaican guy with Medusa-like hair.

Bong

A pipe for smoking weed or opium, where the smoke is filtered through water. Very popular in the Far East, along with playing flutes to live cobras and saying 'Open Sesame' to caves.

Skins/Rizlas

Cigarette papers – every pothead's flexible friend.

Bust

The unexpected arrival of several police officers, waving truncheons to cause maximum confusion while planting evidence.

Eeh-ah-eeh-ah-eeh!

The sound of a police car screeching to a halt on your cat.

Pot Slang

There are many words to describe the use of pot. Here are a few more.

Ganjamuffin

A cake you secretly bake for your girlfriend which causes her to giggle uncontrollably and take her clothes off in restaurants.

Bobby-sox

The sudden appearance of a
policeman, forcing you to hide a
lighted spliff in your sock.

Metrication

A heated argument with a dealer
who is trying to use EEC jargon
to convince you a gram is the same
as an ounce.

Paperless Office

The unwelcome realization while working the night shift that you have run out of cigarette papers.

Paperless Office 2

The subsequent realization that rolling a spliff in a copy of the Financial Times will only set off the smoke alarms.

The Jesus and Mary Chain

Passing around a spliff at Sunday school. This can be turned into an amusing game where everyone sings 'Lord of the Dance' until the music stops, whereupon the one left holding the joint has to smoke the lot.

Pot Pourris

The act of dropping a small chunk of hash into a flowerbed, resulting in two hours of frantic digging like a demented mole.

Shit of Fools

Throwing a bag of oregano into a drug
rehabilitation clinic and waiting for the
fight to start.

Jamaican Jerk Chicken

A Rastafarian who refuses to
smoke anything stronger than
Marlboro Lights.

Scared shitless

The growing realization that you are
running out of hash and your dealer is
still in jail.

Nut-casing

Hiding marijuana in your trousers,
causing dogs and passing junkies
to take an unnatural interest
in your crotch.

Supergrass

The discovery of three kilos of pure Sensimilia in a forgotten Wellington boot. Highly unlikely, of course, but that's what makes it 'super'.

Pot-Noodle

Ordering a Chinese takeaway while stoned, resulting in twelve chicken chow meins and thirty-five portions of prawn crackers arriving at five-minute intervals in the company of an increasingly knackered delivery man.

Grassy Knoll

A place where FBI agents hang out smoking weed when they should be watching the President.

Going Dutch

A weekend trip to Amsterdam beginning with a visit to one of the local 'coffee' shops. Thirty-six hours later you awake on the ferry home, in the company of a prostitute and a donkey.

Potted History...

Cannabis has been used as a drug for over five thousand years and an industrial crop for far longer. Here are a few things you may not know about the world's favourite illegal high.

8000 BC A piece of fabric dating to this time suggests hemp production is one of the oldest industries of all, used to produce rope, fabric, oil and food. Cannabis is only one strain of the plant, but the one which caused most trouble in the early twentieth century.

3700 BC The first recorded use of cannabis, in a book by the Chinese pharmacologist Shen Nung. Stories that he went on to open the first Chinese takeaway and eat himself to death are probably exaggerated.

450 BC The Greek historian Herodotus describes the Scythians throwing hemp onto heated stones and inhaling the fumes. Is this the origin of the term 'stoned'? I don't know, man, quit hassling me!

1150 AD The Moslems start Europe's first paper mill, producing hemp paper. Up until the mid-nineteenth century, more than three-quarters of the world's paper was made from hemp fibre. Mohammed himself accepted the use of cannabis, but not of alcohol – conclusive proof that no religion is ever quite perfect.

1563 Queen Elizabeth I decrees that landowners with sixty acres or more have to grow hemp or face a £5 fine. Nearly 450 years later Queen Elizabeth II has yet to attend her first rave – so much for progress!

1776 The US Declaration of Independence is drafted on hemp paper. Although never smoked, you have to admit the bit about 'the right to bear arms' does sound seriously shit-faced.

1890 Queen Victoria is prescribed tincture of cannabis for period pains by her personal physician, J. R. Reynolds, who calls it 'One of the most valuable medicines we possess.' Unfortunately, he said much the same thing about drilling holes in the skull to relieve migraines.

1900 W. B. Yeats and his lover Maude Gonne use hashish to improve their telepathic powers. Sadly, it prevents the Irish poet and playwright from sensing that not many people understood a blind word he said or wrote.

1925 Cannabis becomes illegal in the UK after agreement of the Geneva International Convention on Narcotics Control, where it is denounced by the Egyptian delegate for making large numbers of his countrymen look 'wide-eyed and stupid' – qualities many a Hollywood starlet would have died for.

1930 Louis Armstrong is arrested in New Orleans for possessing marijuana. The police want to bust him for 'Being a black man in control of a trumpet', but it isn't technically illegal.

1967 On Valentine's Day Jimi Hendrix secretly funds the mailing out of three thousand joints to addresses chosen randomly from the phonebook. When he dies three years later not one of the ungrateful bastards turns up.

1973 President Nixon declares, 'We have turned the corner on drug addiction in America.' Nine months later America turns the corner on him.

1980 Paul McCartney spends ten days in a Japanese prison for marijuana possession. Sadly, he gets off on the more serious charges of 'Forming Wings' and 'Ruining Stevie Wonder's career with "Ebony and Ivory".'

1992 Bill Clinton admits to smoking pot while at university in England but says he 'didn't inhale'. Which is a bit like having an orgasm over someone but claiming you never had sex. Mind you, he said that too.

1999 Politicians fall over themselves to talk about whether or not they have smoked cannabis. Mo Mowlam says she has, William Hague says he has not, and Tony Blair keeps repeating the word 'education', which sounds suspiciously stoned to me.

2000 Respected academic Dr Leslie Iverson suggests pot is less harmful than aspirin. 'Despite the widespread illicit use of cannabis there are very few if any instances of people dying from an overdose,' he says, shortly before choking on a Mars Bar and bursting into flames. (NB: That last bit is probably untrue.)

Growing Tips

Marijuana is a weed, which means it can be grown almost anywhere – well, anywhere the cops and the neighbours aren't looking. Here are a few tips I overheard in the pub.

If **neighbours** start paying undue attention, don't try telling them, 'Weeds have feelings too, man.'

Marijuana plants can grow as high as nine feet, so planting them in a window box may look a tad conspicuous and cause your balcony to collapse onto the flat below.

Building a **bonfire** too close to a marijuana patch may cause flocks of stoned sparrows to plummet out of the sky onto your lawn.

Only **female plants** produce cannabis resin. After fertilization, males just take up space – proof that God is consistent, if nothing else.

Always plant your weeds at least **three feet apart**. You may be able to convince dim policemen they're an optical illusion caused by inhaling the stuff they found inside.

Blackfly and greenfly just love munching on your precious weed. Keep them at bay with a good insecticide; alternatively call in a blind gardener with no sense of smell.

Plant your ganja in **April** for a late summer harvest. Alternatively, plant it in October for a very expensive joke and a roomful of pissed-off junkies.

Weed needs **plenty of light**, around fifteen hours per day – which is about fourteen hours more than the average junkie gets.

Once the female plants start **budding**, they need to be uprooted and dried. This can be done on the floor or in a warm, dark cupboard. Taking them down the laundromat with a bagful of 20p coins is not to be recommended.

Weed plants respond to **music**, growing towards the sound of Bob Marley but turning black and dying over anything by Hanson.

While the cannabis flower is producing resin there may be a **pungent smell**. This can be camouflaged by burning copious amounts of incense. Alternatively, use the traditional method of never, ever washing and growing dreadlocks.

Although weed needs plenty of light to grow, it needs plenty of **darkness** to flower. So, if you get busted and thrown in jail, do try to take your plants with you.

Hydroponics is a method of cultivating plants indoors without the use of soil. It works fine for cannabis, but costs a small fortune and turns your hippy trippy love den into a sixth-form science lab.

Famous Potheads

It's not just Christian martyrs who were stoned to death. Most of these guys were too.

Keith Moon (1946–1978)

Former drummer with the Who, Keith did more drugs than a Colombian pharmacist. On one occasion he challenged Ringo Starr and Mother Theresa to a naked drumming competition in his swimming pool . . . or at least he thought he did.

Dylan from The Magic Roundabout

How this permanently stoned bunny ever made it on to a children's programme is a mystery. Dylan used to hang around the magic garden waiting for his dealer, Mr McHenry. He was sensationally sacked in 1974 after encouraging Parsley the Lion to smoke most of the Herb Garden.

Bob Marley (1945–1981)

A lifelong ganja user, which led to his distinctive laid-back musical style. Still, with songs like 'Buffalo Solider', 'Hooligan' and 'I shot the Sheriff' you have to be grateful he was too stoned to handle a real gun.

42

Galileo (1564–1642)

The Italian astrologer reputedly discovered pot while looking for the centre of the universe. After that, he pretty much lost interest in everything, taking the secret of the electric car, the time machine and the never-ending Mars Bar to the grave with him.

Jim Morrison

Another legendary pothead, Jim went on more trips than Buster Keaton at an ice rink. Although acid was his favourite airline, he often used dope as an undercarriage, sadly reaching the departure lounge in 1971. Even today fans of his music have little or no idea the 60s are over.

Samuel Taylor Coleridge (1772–1834)

Primarily an opium user, the celebrated poet was also known to experiment with cannabis. The albatross in 'Rime of the Ancient Mariner' is widely thought to refer to his dealer, although what the hell 'Kubla Khan' is about is anyone's guess.

Joan of Arc

During her trial in 1431, Joan was
accused of using 'witch drugs' to
invoke her mystical voices. She was
subsequently burned at the stake,
without a roach.

Bill Hicks

was as outspoken about drugs as everything else. 'Not only do I think pot should be legalized,' he said, 'it should be mandatory.' Sadly, he died of cancer in 1994 and was last reported sharing a spliff with St Peter.

Sean Ryder

The frontman of Black Grape and the Happy Mondays is miraculously still alive and performing despite consuming more drugs per day than a sick hippo. Nevertheless, with his incomprehensible lyrics and glazed appearance, he remains a hero to millions who can't be arsed to find a better one.

Noel Gallagher

The songwriting half of Oasis famously
said that 'smoking cannabis is as
normal as having a cup of tea'. 'That's
as maybe,' replied the manager of the
Saffron Walden Tea Rooms, 'but you'll
have to do your skinning up outside,
you young scallywag.'

ET

Introduced to pot by Drew Barrymore,
out-takes from the movie clearly show
him repeating the words 'ET . . .
home-grown'. His parents promptly
sued Stephen Spielberg for $23 million
before settling in Palm Springs. ET
bounced in and out of rehab, his
career reaching rock bottom with the
infamous porno movie ET2 – 'It's not
just his finger that glows.' Currently
works for BT.

Carl Sagan (1934–1996)

The renowned physicist was on the board of the National Organisation for the reform of Marijuana Laws (NORML). He also co-wrote the movie *Contact*, perhaps the best argument for not doing pot ever invented.

Haile Selassie

Though not a pothead himself, the ex-ruler of Ethiopia (real name Ras Tafari) was the reluctant figurehead of the Rastafarians, who believe marijuana is a sacred herb. Admittedly, this is a bit like believing beer is an archangel but hey, it sure beats Sunday School.

Whitney Houston

In May 2000, the soul diva was busted at a Hawaiian airport for carrying half an ounce of weed. When she was released without charge the authorities were accused of favouritism. 'It was only a small amount,' said a spokesman, 'whereas her husband was carrying a very big gun.'

You know you're doing too much pot when...

The symptoms of doing too much dope are obvious to all but the user. If you can recognize any of these, it's time to pause between rolling.

When invited to phone a friend on
Who Wants to be a Millionaire,
the only person you can think of is
your dealer and his answer to every
question is, 'OK, but this is from my
own personal stash, you
understand. . .'

You can talk for twenty minutes on the
subject of pepperoni.

You look in the mirror and see luggage.

You wear the same T-shirt so long the logo transfers to your chest.

You start buying Rizlas in bulk, direct from the depot.

You're smoking so much the cat thinks
he's Hitler and annexes the cat-flap.

The local all-you-can-eat restaurant
hires a hitman.

You buy the latest Delia Smith cookbook and have to eat it in the shop.

During a Commons debate on drug raids, you interrupt the Home Secretary to ask him what they do with the leftovers.

Your cleaner enters the house making the sign of the cross.

You are arrested as part of a police campaign called 'Operation Predictable Junkie'.

All your anecdotes begin with the words 'There was this one time when I was stoned…'

You never get any mail, as every time the postman opens the letterbox he forgets why he came.

You start chewing five minutes before food arrives.

There's a photo of you hanging in the local Pizza Hut under the heading 'This guy keeps us and the anchovy fishermen of northern Spain in business.'

Your accountant queries your monthly payments to 'The Brixton Coffee Company.'

Safety Tips

Smoking pot is dangerous to more than your reputation. Following these simple tips will ensure a safe junkie remains a happy one.

Never smoke dope before sex. It's like wearing the condom over your brain. Say, that's not a bad idea . . .

Try to live within a mile of a corner shop, bakery or KFC – 10 per cent of potheads may eat themselves to death by the age of thirty, but over 50 per cent die while trying to fly across dual carriageways.

Never roll up while the police are actually in the process of frisking you.

Beware of great ideas you have while stoned. Cars cannot be made to run on curry, and never washing your penis will not make it grow.

Posh potheads – try not to draw attention to yourself. If you must ask Harrods to deliver your Rizlas don't add, 'Oh, and five hundred Mars Bars, my good man!'

When buying hash, always trust your nose. The aroma you're looking for is part henna, part cannabis resin and part Rastafarian crotch (where it's been hidden for the best part of a fortnight). Remember, they call it 'shit' for a reason!

Weed plants can be camouflaged by attaching plastic tomatoes to the branches. NB: don't try attaching pineapples, melons or coconuts – the police may be corrupt, but they ain't stupid.

Beware of DIY ideas you have while stoned. One nail will not hold up a supporting wall and Ikea coffee tables are no substitute for real skateboards.

In the event of being prosecuted for possession, remember 'Shit happens' is not a valid legal defence as to how an ounce of it wound up in your car.

Smoking a joint kills around seven hundred brain calls. Mind you, watching Ready Steady Cook kills twice that many and also ruins your appetite.

Under the influence of dope people often say things they later regret – still at least we didn't blow £2.50 on some lame-arse joke book, eh, sucker?

Beware of great fashion ideas you have while stoned. Wearing the same black jeans and Metallica T-shirt for three years is not a fashion statement, it's a health hazard.

Policemen – beware of your sniffer dogs developing a drug habit. Early warning signs include sitting around the kennel all day in their own excrement and eating two hundredweight of Winalot.

Cannabis contains around four times as many cancer-causing chemicals as ordinary tobacco. However, given you've got to go sometime, it might as well be on a magic carpet with a mouthful of Hula Hoops.

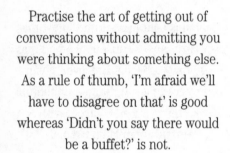

Practise the art of getting out of
conversations without admitting you
were thinking about something else.
As a rule of thumb, 'I'm afraid we'll
have to disagree on that' is good
whereas 'Didn't you say there would
be a buffet?' is not.

In the event of being busted, never try to make a run for it. There's nothing funnier than twelve junkies bouncing off walls like marbles trying to find the doorway, while policemen sit around smoking the evidence.

The Pottery

There is so much disinformation about pot that certain myths have sprung up. Here are some of the more dangerous ones.

Smoking pot will not help you to fly. It can, however, put your bank account in freefall.

Astronauts are not potheads. They maintain the appearance of weightlessness due to the absence of gravity in outer space. Oh, and while we're at it, there is no crack on Mars.

If you play a Bee Gees album backwards while stoned, it does not sound like a flock of sheep being taken from behind. In actual fact you don't have to play it backwards … or be stoned.

There is no proof the ancient Egyptians were potheads. The fact that they called dead people 'mummies', built giant stone Toblerones in the desert and worshipped gods with the heads of animals is probably down to boredom.

The Children of Israel did not wander in the desert for forty years because they were stoned, looking for a KFC or on the run from the police. According to biblical sources, they were in fact searching for the Promised Land.

In 1941 Henry Ford, the automobile king, constructed a car from reinforced hemp resin, running on hemp-based ethanol. It was scrapped because petrol engines became cheaper, not because the car consumed five hundred gallons a day and insisted on stopping at every service station for a snack.

77

The BBC has constantly denied that some of its best loved children's characters are hopeless potheads. 'Bagpuss was always that lazy,' explained a spokesman, 'and Bill and Ben used to talk bollocks long before they were introduced to Little Weed.'

During the filming of *Apocalypse Now* the crew were not too stoned to notice Martin Sheen having a heart attack or Marlon Brando eating most of the rainforest. Neither does this explain the movie being so goddamn long.

The term dope does not derive from the Department of Political Engineering, formed by MI5 in 1933 to create a race of genetically superior politicians. Neither was DOPE disbanded in the 60s after only managing to come up with John Major.

Although Rastafarians follow the instructions in Genesis and Exodus to 'eat the herb of the field' and 'eat every herb of the land' this is not a valid legal defence for possession. Neither can the story of Gideon bringing down the walls of Jericho be used to justify owning a car stereo that registers on the Richter scale.

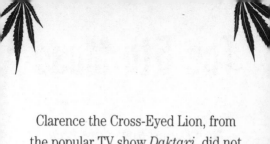

Clarence the Cross-Eyed Lion, from the popular TV show *Daktari*, did not develop his appearance through eating copious amounts of Botswanan home-grown. Neither was he packed off to animal rehab where he shared a padded enclosure with Skippy the Bush Kangaroo and the cast of *Michael Bentine's Potty Time*.

The 5th Muse

Many great lines have been written while under the influence of pot. Here are the alleged original versions before the author sobered up and changed them to something more acceptable.

'One small spliff for man
One giant Wagon Wheel for mankind'

Neil Armstrong after too much
moon-dust

'If you can keep your head when all
    about you
Are losing theirs,
You ought to try Skunk, bwoy,
It's well wicked!'

Rudyard Kipling – also made
exceedingly good cake

'The road to hell is paved with oregano'
  Anon but surprisingly true

'Now, I know what you're thinking
Did he smoke six spliffs or only five?
Well, to be perfectly honest, I'm not quite
  sure…
So, do you feel hungry, punk?'
  Clint Eastwood – presumably missing
  those Spaghetti Westerns

'Imagine there's no Rizlas
It's easy if you try'
John Lennon – shortly before sending
Yoko out to get some

'It is easier for a camel to pass through the
eye of a needle
Than for a pothead to pass a KFC without
going in…'
Jesus Christ – allegedly

'I wandered lonely as a cloud
That floats on high, so soft and pure,
When all at once I saw a pig
Oh shit, I'm busted now for sure…'

*William Wordsworth – finding fun in
the Lake District despite foot and mouth*

'I know I have the body of a weak and
    feeble woman
But I can smoke any of you bastards under
    the table'

*Elizabeth I, shortly after Raleigh
    introduced her to cannabis*

'What's new, pussycat?
Whoahhhhhhh!
What's new, pussycat?
Whoahhhhhh!'
*Tom Jones after touching the green,
green grass of home*

'I have nothing to declare but
my incoherence'
*Oscar Wilde, witty even while
whammied*

Things to say when the police call

Police attention is an occupational hazard of using dope. Best have a few excuses up your sleeve, then . . .

'No, honestly, officer, I always keep my front room full of Wagon Wheels.'

'I have to smoke pot for a medical condition, and my doctor will confirm it … He's lying over there eating the curtains.'

'If you must know, I've been collecting Rizlas for nigh on thirty years.'

'Well, the man down the garden centre
assured me it was a Jamaican cactus.'

'That funny smell? It's just my new
aftershave – Bob Marley's Obsession.'

'I'm rehearsing for the onset of senile dementia.'

'I wanted to see if junkies really did smell worse than other mammals.'

'I'd be quite happy to answer your questions, officer – but the two elephants will have to wait outside with the unicorn.'

'That suspicious bulge in my trousers? It must be seeing you in that helmet…'

'Sorry about all the smoke – I was cooking a roast. Actually, just a couple of steaks – not even a proper joint, really . . . All right, I'll come quietly.'

'All right – nobody moves or the pig gets it!' (NB: Best be holding a gun when you say this, as waving a Twix rarely has the same effect.)

'Oh, you must want the Rastafarians who live next door. Just follow the suspicious smell and the sound of machine-gun fire.'

'I demand to see my lawyer. No, wait, you know that guy who got OJ Simpson off? I demand to see him.'

'Listen, what say we split the weed, make a chocolate cake, and forget about the whole thing?' (NB: You'd be surprised how often this works.)

Jokes that sound funny when you're stoned

How many penguins does it take to build a lighthouse?

None, alligators can't fly.

**What do you get if you cross
Charlie Dimmock with a pothead?**

One hell of a garden.

Two potheads walk in to a bar and
order three bags of crisps and a
twelve-inch pianist. 'Hey, wasn't that
the punchline?' asks the first.
'Search me,' says the other, 'I was over
there shagging the fruit machine…'

What's the difference between a junkie and an ISA?

The ISA will eventually mature and make money.

How do you get a one-armed junkie out of a tree?

Throw him a spliff.

How many potheads does it take to change a lightbulb?

Who cares, man, it was too bright in here anyway…

Did you hear about the junkie who couldn't afford weed so he tried smoking curry powder?

Apparently, he's in a Korma.

Two potheads are lying by the side of the road when a police car speeds by at 100 m.p.h., lights and alarms at full tilt. Five minutes later one turns to the other and says, 'My God, I thought they'd never leave.'

What's the definition of boredom?
Two junkies discussing what they did last summer.

Knock knock.

Er . . . Who's there?

Julio.

Julio who?

What?

Well, you started it!

Then who am I?

Who?

What?

(Ad infinitum.)

Diary of a Dopehead

Mike Anderiesz was a promising writer and journalist before researching pot for the purposes of writing a book. This is the tragic account of his final months.

January Had my first joint today. Euch! Judging by this, the 60s were well over-rated. My girlfriend says it makes me talk rubbish … she's so cute. Can't wait till we're married.

February Book's going well, the research is fascinating. My friend Will says that tobacco was discovered by accident after Walter Raleigh was ripped off by an unscrupulous Apache dealer named Dances with Weeds. Which reminds me, must get some more…

March My editor told me that Hawaiian shirts and shades aren't in the office dress code. Jesus, what a square – reminds me of my girlfriend, whom I'm supposed to be marrying next month. Better order up some weed for the stag night, I guess.

May Whoo, that was good shit! What month is it anyway? Oh right … better call the girl and explain why I missed the wedding. Just roll one more joint before I go …

June The cow left me. Sod it, she never understood me anyway … not like my dealer. Wish he was a woman and didn't smell quite so bad. Oops, late for our rendezvous. He says he'll be wearing black, carrying a big-ass blunt and being pursued by police … as usual.

July I seem to have lost my job. Just as well, as I can't remember where the office is. Never mind, it gives me a chance to get my music career off the ground. I've written this song called 'Twenty-Four Mars Bars from Tulsa' – it's got hit written all over it.

August No it hasn't. The record company said it sounded like two junkies repeating the word 'Mars Bar' into a microphone. Bullshit! There were at least three of us. Never mind, I'm working on a website now – it's called **www.legalisecannabisoratleastsendussome.com**, the papers are going to love it.

September No they didn't. Which is a pity because my landlord is demanding more rent after my last cheque bounced higher than a Jamaican on a pogo stick. Damn, if I don't make some money soon I'm in trouble. Ah … that's better.

October I am evicted and forced to share a flat with seven Rastafarians and their machetes. We have lost all sense of time. Last night we watched the Cartoon Network for thirteen hours before running out of weed and having to smoke our own dreadlocks.

November We've decided to grow dope commercially. We found a book called *The Little Book of Pot* which has a chapter on growing tips that we intend to follow religiously. Now we're cooking, bwoy!

December Damn, this is the worst book ever. All the plants died and the police are watching the house. It's like the guy who wrote it didn't know anything about pot at all. Still, he has an interesting tip about being able to fly. Worth a try, eh?

Mike was last seen in the Brixton area, plummeting fast. His family wish it to be known that he still owes them money.

Pothead Recipes

Potted Shrimps Take five tiger prawns and add 1 tsp of freshly made aïoli. Sprinkle with salt and vinegar crisps and chocolate fudge brownies. Oh, and make some sandwiches too…

Broiled Cabbage Smoke five joints and then fall asleep in a sauna.

Rastafarian Rice Mix 1lb of Basmati rice with 1oz of purest Sensimilia grass. Then try to find the plates, or the kitchen for that matter…

Baked Alaskan An Eskimo dish consisting of ice-cream rolled in marijuana. Sadly, not as tasty as it sounds.

Pot au Vin Stuff a chicken with Wagon Wheels. Drink the wine while you're waiting for the chocolate to melt.

Fried Seaweed Smoke five joints at the beach and then fall asleep on the hood of your car.

What music sounds like when you're stoned

Philip Glass

Stoned *It's like the more you hear it, the deeper it sounds.*

Later Is every track exactly the same as the last one?

Mike Oldfield

Stoned *Wow, I really have to get his new album.*

Later Well, that's another $15 down the crapper.

The Happy Mondays

Stoned *All dance music should sound like this.*

Later Does anyone have the faintest idea what they're on about?

Pink Floyd

Stoned *They seem to understand exactly how I'm feeling.*

> **Later** I really have to get out more.

Laurie Anderson

Stoned *She was so far ahead of her time.*

> **Later** Isn't this playing at the wrong speed?

Bob Marley

Stoned *You know I could be black if I wanted to.*

       Later Actually, I think it was the dope that killed him.

Movies to watch when you're stoned

Saving Private Ryan

Oh no . . . Tom Hanks got shot!
War is hell, man.

The Godfather

I've seen this movie so many times and
it's still ... Aghhhh!!! A dead horse!

Chocolat
Would somebody turn this thing off
before I eat myself to death!

Ghandi
Could anyone else murder an Indian?

Yentl
I think we're going to need
a lot more dope…

Oranges are not the only fruit
You know, they've got a point, dude…

Pot songs

'Smoke Gets In Your Eyes'
Brian Ferry recalls the time he got within six feet of the Rolling Stones.

'Puff the Magic Dragon'
A mythical Jamaican beast that used to steal ganja. When spotted, the villagers would scare it away with sticks – hence the expression 'chasing the dragon'.

'Ding Dong Verily I'm High'

Say what you like about bell-ringers,
they sure know how to party.

'The Long and Winding Road'

That leads to nowhere in particular.

'Three Spliffs to Heaven'

Step 1: You find a girl to love
Step 2: She falls in love with you
Step 3: Do you want a shag or not?

'Killing me Softly with his Bong'

The Fugees recall how much pot
the producer smoked during the
recording session.

How stoned are you?

No. of joints   *Topic of conversation*

1–3   'Hey, I'm going to order a pizza
with extra extra anchovies?'

4–5   'I'm not sure I like the way that
anchovy is looking at me…'

6–8 'Say . . . what about listening to some music and then giving me some of that fish love?'

9–10 'Hey, baby, rest those gills – this is the best guitar solo ever...'

11+ 'Look, quit hassling and let me sleep. Jeez, we're not married, you friggin' sardine-substitute.'

Mike Anderiesz is a man on a mission, unfortunately since being introduced to Pot he has forgotten what that mission is and now wanders the world fighting crime, righting injustice and boring the pants off people at parties. He has written extensively on the subject of drugs, including the junky style-guide *The Lion, the Spliff and the Wardrobe* and the controversial children's cartoon *Dopemon – Gotta smoke 'em all!* He is currently being sued by Jasmine Birtles, Russell Michaels and Will Rodgers for neglecting to give them due credit and also for stealing their cutlery.

"I will fight till my dying breath for freedom…" he memorably told Nelson Mandela "…Oh, and Mars Bars." he added, not quite so memorably.

128